Heart Tales

A Collection of Stories from a Child's Heart

Written and illustrated by Jean-Marie Hamel

Silver Forest Publishing
P.O. Box 3520
Evergreen, Colorado 80439

ISBN 0-929684-50-8

*With love and gratitude to
my Mother and Father
and John-Roger*

In honor and
celebration of the
little child that
lives inside
each one of us.

Heart Tales

Froggy Friends

There were two froggy friends named Freda and Frank,
Who had a big surprise down by the river bank.

One day while they were hopping around,
A large tub of cream on the ground they found.

They fell in the tub, which wasn't their plan,
But that's how froggy friends lessons began.

"I'll never get out,"
Frank began to shout,

"I'm a loser, defeated,"
He echoed, repeated.

So, Frank gave up and began to drown,
He sank to the bottom turned upside down.

But Freda believed, she knew she'd get out,
She trusted herself without any doubt.

"You can only go as far,
As the kind of frog you think you are."

"I'm confident, I'm a winner,
I'll be out of here in time for dinner."

Around and around she swam 'til she found,
Cream churns to butter, pound by pound.

She hopped right out, reached back in,
Snatching up Frank by the scruff of his skin.

Frank said to Freda, with a ribbeting grin,
"Thank-you dear friend, I wasn't tuned in."

"Now I know that belief comes from within,
I'll remember this day knowing I can win."

The two froggy friends hugged and smiled,
Enjoyed their freedom for a long, long while.

They dined upon a bed of moss,
On fresh flies washed in butter sauce.

Savored each and every tidbit,
In the sun
      On the bank
         Of the River
            Ribbet.

 **WHO-O ARE YOU?**

I am as confident as I can be,
Loving myself and believing in me.

Dancing Doris Duck

Doris Duck was swimming one day,
In the clear, cool, blue Bay of Biscay.

Her friend Billy Blue Jay was flying nearby,
Squawkin' his songs to the faraway sky.

Timmie the Turtle moved slowly along,
Playing his flute, song after song.

Doris got the rhythm and wanted to dance,
But why appear silly, why take the chance?

"I couldn't, I wouldn't, I shouldn't!" she cried,
"No duck in my family ever has tried."

"Ducks waddle, they wiggle, they're not meant to dance!"
But Timmie convinced her, she must take a chance.

Sayin' "Step right up and be my guest,
You just dance and I'll do the rest!"

The music was sweet, it had a great beat,
And Doris discovered she had dancin' feet.

She followed the music she heard inside,
Spread her wings and danced with pride.

She was so happy and felt so free,
She kicked up her heels and quacked, "Look at me!"

WHO-O ARE YOU?

I am joyfully learning to dance,
Trying new things and taking a chance.

Edith's Best Friend

Edith Earthworm was living alone,
And every day she'd grumble and moan.

"Dull and lank, simple and plain,
I'm not good enough," she'd complain.

She didn't think she was worth a lot,
And what she thought was what she got.

She didn't believe she was any good,
So there was no reason anybody else should.

Her tunnels were spotless, but that didn't matter,
She knew that someone's were smoother or fatter.

She spent her days beneath the damp ground,
She never went out, she wore her best frown.

One day, she chose to lift her head,
Out of the dirt and look up instead.

She saw a worm three inches away,
And the worm was pretty to her dismay.

Edith said, "I wish I could be,
Just like you, instead of me."

The other worm giggled, "You're as pretty as me,
Silly, you're my other half, don't you see?"

What Edith had thought were separate parts,
Were joined in the middle by a great big heart.

Edith smiled proudly then shouted with glee,
"What I see in others is a reflection of me!"

Now, her best buddy is her other end,
Finding herself, Edith found a friend.

 **WHO-O ARE YOU?**

I am worthy and accepting of me,
Happily becoming all I can be.

Miss Mattie's Bouquet

One morning Miss Mattie woke with a hunch,
To pick some flowers to put in a bunch.

She doubted her choice and couldn't begin,
Mattie felt confused—what a state she was in!

She plucked off the petals of a daisy with skill,
Saying, "Maybe I won't pick, maybe I will."

Then, she asked for help from her friend Toad,
As he pedaled his bike down the winding road.

Toad rarely gave advice, he was willing to now,
He paused on his travels and said he knew how.

"Choices I make from my heart,
Are honest ones and awfully smart."

"Myself, I use the Toad-Choosing Trick,
It makes all decisions easy and quick."

"I close my eyes to see what's true
Pretend I know just what to do."

"Then open my eyes and I will see,
What the answer to my question will be."

Mattie shut her eyes, just as he said,
While tulips and daffodils danced in her head.

Then, blinking, squealing "Yes!" in a voice,
Telling Toad she had made her choice.

So, she spent the day, picking a bouquet,
Of lovely flowers that brightened her day.

Tulips, pansies, and buttercups,
Daffodils, daisies, and johnnie-jump-ups.

Toad waved good-bye and felt so pleased,
Knowing Mattie could now make choices with ease.

WHO-O ARE YOU?

I am making a wise choice,
Believing in my very own voice.

Caterpillar and Butterfly

Upon one time, a story was told,
Of a caterpillar, who grew very old.

He didn't like change, he hated new things,
To yesterday's memories he chose to cling.

Scared of thunder, scared of lightning,
Scared of bug-a-boos that are frightening.

He stayed to himself, complained everyday,
Because he'd always done it that way.

"Quite safe, thank-you," so he would say,
While always on the same pathway.

"I'm very familiar with my own way,
Because I've always done it this way."

Lifting his head, he spied in the sky,
A beauteous butterfly fluttering by.

"Hey there, butterfly soaring around,
Everyone knows that home's on the ground."

"I'd never feel safe, as a matter-of-fact,
I'd never have wings to fly like that."

Butterfly smiled at him down below,
"I suppose," she said, "It's important to know,"

"To never say never, it isn't so strange,
One thing you can count on in life is change."

Caterpillar frowned, grumbled, protested,
Crawled back to cocoon, as usual, he rested.

Leaves left unnibbled, even lunch became boring,
He dreamt of a dragonfly while he was snoring.

Then, the miracle began to unfold,
He woke as a butterfly, winged with gold.

Soaring, exploring, able to see,
Changes in life can set us free.

Supported by sky, as safe as can be,
He looks at the world quite differently.

WHO-O ARE YOU?

I am easily changing in my own way,
Safely growing up day by day.

The Hann Family Clan

On a midnight walk that the Hann family took,
They all came away with a new outlook.

Momma Hann, Daddy Hann, and four children too,
Were walking in the woods right next to the zoo.

Hilary, Henry, and Helen Hann,
Joined Harry to make up the Hann family clan.

Midpath, in blackness, an elephant stood,
But midnight's too dark to see very good.

Daddy grabbed its tail and said, "I hope,
This thing in my hand is the end of a rope."

Momma felt its leg and said, "It seems to me,
We are up against the trunk of a tree."

Hilary rubbed its belly and said, "I recall,
This feels like the bricks in a wall."

Henry felt its ear and said to his clan,
"I'm certain, for sure, this is a huge fan."

Touching its tusk, Helen turned around,
"It's a gigantic spear that we have found."

Harry grabbed its nose and screamed with fright,
"Run for your lives and hide out-of-sight!"

"It's not what you think, it's a monstrous snake
Run quickly now, for safety's sake!"

They scampered and scurried out of the way,
To come back tomorrow in clear light of day.

All of the family had misunderstood,
'Cause there stood an elephant in the woods.

Each made his decision with part of the facts,
What fact one Hann knew, the other one lacked.

The elephant smiled at the Hann family clan,
They laughed and the elephant rides began.

WHO-O ARE YOU?

I am clearly seeing with joy in my heart,
The whole is more than the sum of each part.

Darrell's Dog-Gone Christmas Tree

"What a wonderful Christmas tree this will be!"
Darrell Dog shouted through the forest, "Yippie!"

He raised his axe and began to chop,
The tree didn't fall and Darrell Dog stopped.

"I'll never be able to chop this tree,
I give up, I'm defeated, poor-little-me."

A redbird named Robert swooped down from the tree,
As sassy and saucy as street-wise could be.

"I know at times it seems difficult,
If you give up now, you won't get results."

"When you think you can't, that's when you must,
Stand tall, wag your tail, and always trust."

"Believe in yourself and be the very best,
Stay true to yourself, in yourself invest."

Darrell used these words to his benefit,
Raised his axe and yelled, "I'll do it!"

"I'll finish the job that I have begun!"
He chopped the tree and even had fun.

The pine tree wobbled, then fell with a crash,
Then it all came clear to Darrell in a flash.

"I almost gave up before I was done,
My patience was nothing, and trust, I had none."

"I stuck to my goal, staying on track,
All of my confidence soon came back."

"I'll have popcorn and redbirds on my Christmas tree,
I believe in myself, Merry Christmas, Yippie!"

WHO-O ARE YOU?

I am growing in confidence with each new test,
Stretching to reach my personal best.

Silver Forest Publishing

P.O. Box 3520
Evergreen, Colorado 80439
1-800-669-5755

Silver Forest Publishing is proud to present **Heart Tales.** Our philosophy is to bring you work of the highest quality. We are very interested in your comments and suggestions. Please write or call us. Our goal is to bring greater upliftment to the world in which we live.

Thank-you,

Silver Forest Publishing